This book belongs to:

....

For
Seb,
Pippa
and
Harry

OXFORD
UNIVERSITY PRESS

Great Clarendon Street, Oxford OX2 6DP

Oxford University Press is a department of the University of Oxford.
It furthers the University's objective of excellence in research, scholarship,
and education by publishing worldwide. Oxford is a registered trade mark
of Oxford University Press in the UK and in certain other countries

Text and illustration copyright © Tim Hopgood 2019

The moral rights of the author have been asserted

Database right Oxford University Press (maker)

First published 2019
First published in this edition 2020

British Library Cataloguing in Publication Data
Data available

ISBN: 978-0-19-276759-2

10 9 8 7 6 5 4 3

Printed in China

Paper used in the production of this book is a natural, recyclable product
made from wood grown in sustainable forests. The manufacturing process
conforms to the environmental regulations of the country of origin.

CYRiL

THE LONELY CLOUD

tim hopgood

OXFORD
UNIVERSITY PRESS

'Let's have a picnic!'

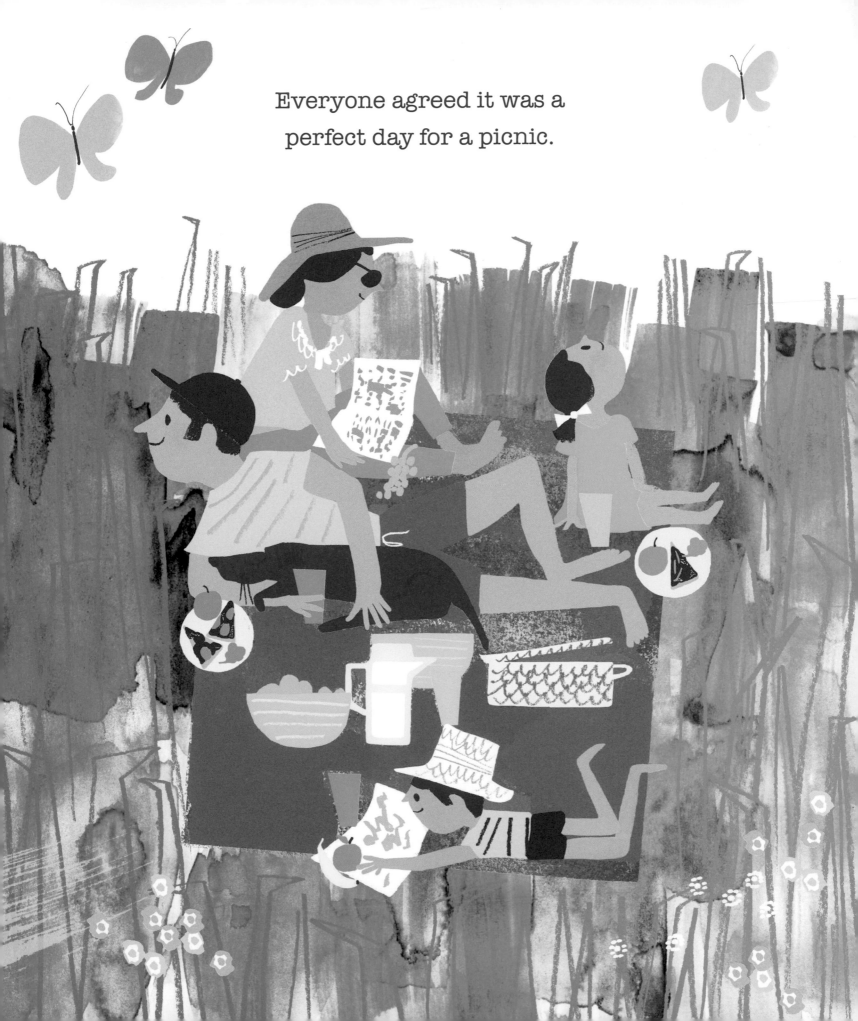

Everyone agreed it was a
perfect day for a picnic.

At least it was until Cyril turned up.

It was sad but true, no one was ever pleased to see Cyril.

He was always being blamed for ruining everyone's fun.

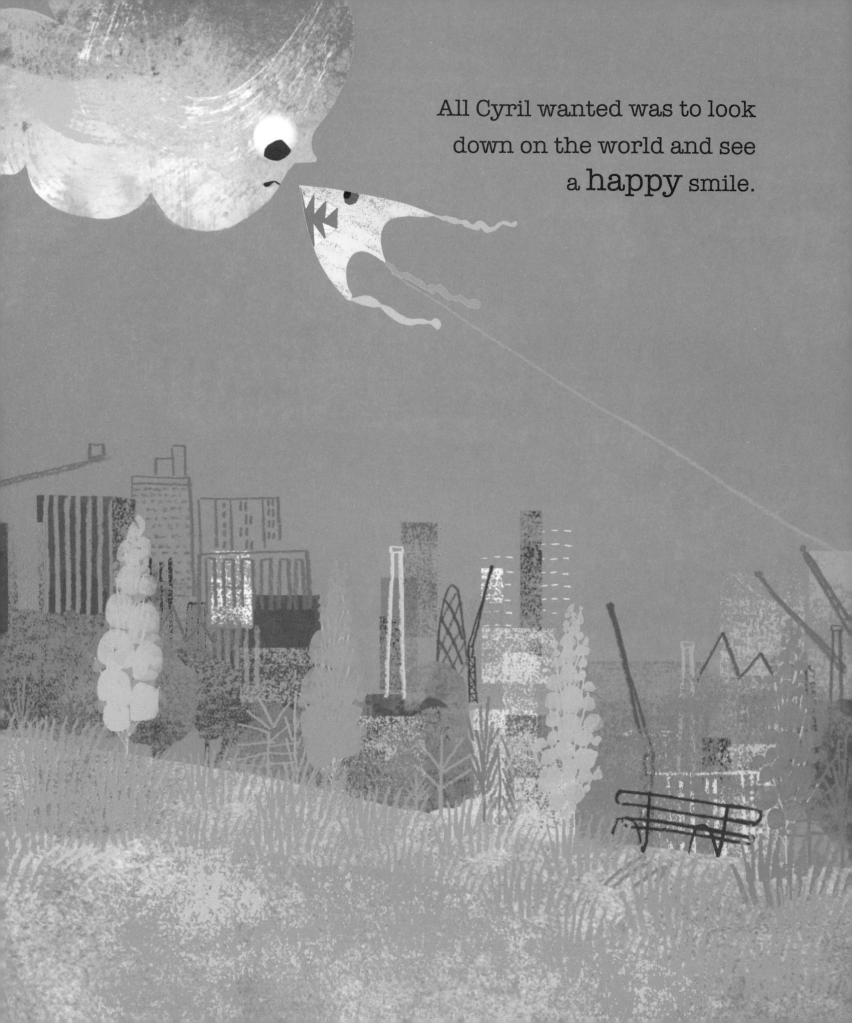

All Cyril wanted was to look down on the world and see a **happy** smile.

The trouble was, he knew what
everyone was thinking . . .

*I wish that cloud
would go away!*

So that's exactly
what he did.

Cyril drifted far, far away in search of a friendly face.

He floated over farmland, rivers and bridges . . .

above towns
and famous cities . . .

and over the **OCEAN** too!

As Cyril drifted across
the water he gradually
became bigger . . .

and
bigger!

Eventually Cyril came to a new land.

The ground was **baking** hot.

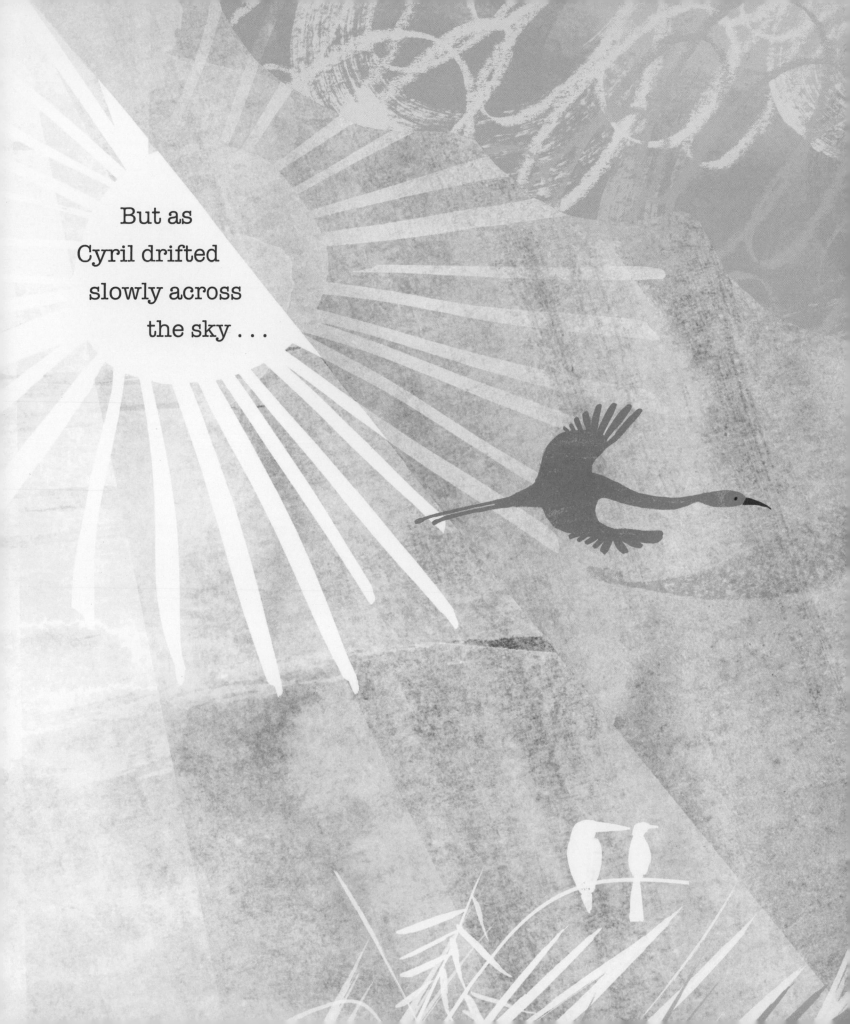

But as
Cyril drifted
slowly across
the sky . . .

his **huge** shadow cooled the earth.

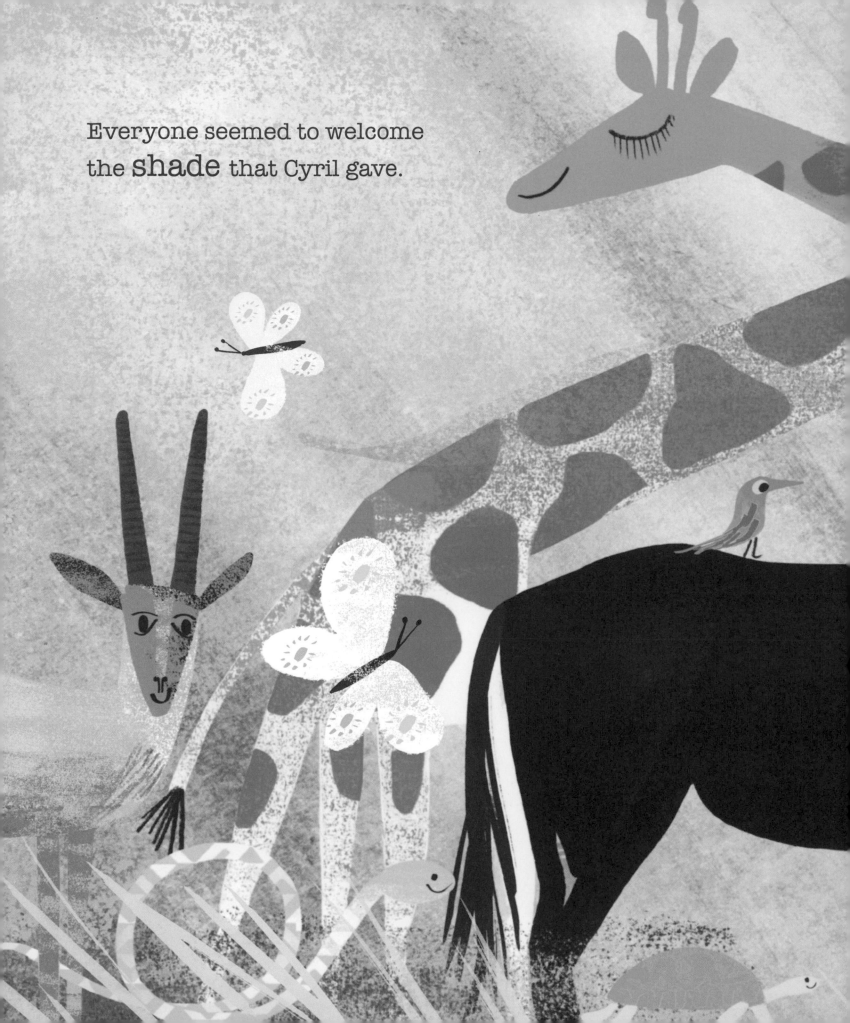

Everyone seemed to welcome the **shade** that Cyril gave.

This made
Cyril feel
so happy
that he cried.

Not tears of
sadness . . .

but big,
big tears of
glorious **joy**!

As Cyril's tears soaked the land,
everything seemed to smile!

And that
was all
Cyril
had ever
wanted . . .

to look
down
on the
world
and
see a
happy
smile.